praise for *Everybody Can Dance!*

"The musicality and boogie beat of Kara Navolio's verse is pitch-perfect. *Everybody Can Dance!* is a joyful ode to dancing feet. Kara has written a little book of inspiration that celebrates our differences and the concept that everybody is one."

—Andrea Alban, author of *The Happiness Tree* and *Anya's War*

"*Everybody Can Dance!* is a joyous celebration of what it means to be human. Endowed with our personal journey, our heartbeat, and life's inner spark, we are all driven to move. The rhythm, hope, and audacious jubilation of this melodious piece brings forth an ear-to-ear smile, as it reminds us that each and every one of us deserves to dance, can dance, and should dance."

—Tonya Amos, Artistic Director, Grown Women Dance Collective, and Alvin Ailey American Dance Center Scholarship Awardee

"Kara Navolio has written a beautiful children's book that brings you on a whimsical journey of musical exploration through dance. It truly gets the rhythm in your bones flowing! Dance allows you to express and communicate using your body as the instrument. *Everybody Can Dance!* shows us that dance is a wonderful way to bring people together. Dance puts smiles on faces and happiness in hearts and should be enjoyed by everyone."

—Erica Pecho, Dance Instructor at The Dance House Napa Valley

Everybody Can Dance!

written by Kara Navolio

illustrated by Ruth-Mary Smith

B Brandylane
Publishers, Inc.

ISBN: 978-1-947860-36-0
LCCN: 2019931247

Designed by Michael Hardison
Project managed by Christina Kann

Printed in the United States of America

Published by
Brandylane Publishers, Inc.
5 S. 1st Street
Richmond, Virginia 23219

Brandylane
Publishers, Inc.
Publishing books since 1985

brandylanepublishers.com

For Bela and her students, who provided the spark;
and Emily, who brought the joy of dance into my life.

~KN

For all my family—
Dave, Jasmin, Kiralee, and Stella—
thanks for supporting my sketching.

~RMS

The music starts. You feel the beat.

You clap your hands and tap your feet.

Everybody can dance!

You can glide or slide,
    whether big or small.

You can swish or sway
    whether short or tall.

Shuffle and stomp

or shimmy and shake.

waltz or hop;

you have what it takes.

Everybody

twist and twirl!

Some people learn to dance on wheels.

Some people tap on toes and heels.

Dancers can spin on hands or heads.

Dancers can sway, healing in beds.

Everybody
whizz and whirl!

Prefer to dance with boys or girls?

Prefer to leap or practice twirls?

Boogie alone or jive in groups.

Lead your partner 'round in loops.

Everybody
swoosh and swirl!

You can dance at home or perform on stage.

You can take a class at any age.

So make some music; play a song.

Create some moves and groove along.

Everybody

can dance!

Styles of Dance

Can you find these styles of dance in the illustrations?

AFRICAN JAZZ blends the lively beats of Caribbean or African music with jazz dance. Dancers often turn, jump, and coordinate steps with partners.

BALLET involves graceful swaying, spinning, and leaping to classical music. Dancers wear tights and soft shoes like slippers; female ballerinas often wear tutus or flowing dresses and hard pointe shoes to dance on their toes.

BALLROOM dance features partners carefully following patterns of steps. Each ballroom dance has a different pattern of movements. Some examples of ballroom dances are the cha-cha, waltz, and tango.

BELLY DANCE is a solo dance that involves slow movements of the belly and fast shimmies of the hips to music that comes from the Middle East. Dancers might also use finger cymbals or long pieces of fabric as props.

BOLLYWOOD dance is featured in movies from India. This kind of dance combines a mixture of traditional dance moves from Indian culture with modern western jazz styles. Dancers use intricate hand movements and wear colorful, beaded costumes.

CONTEMPORARY dance combines elements of ballet, modern, and jazz and often incorporates dance styles from around the world. Dancers' movements usually evoke strong emotions.

COUNTRY WESTERN dance is performed to country music. Dancers usually wear cowboy boots and cowboy hats. They might face each other in two lines or dance in pairs, gliding across the floor.

FLAMENCO dance originated in Spain. Dancers tell stories of the joy and hardships of life with stomping, clapping, and expressive movements accompanied by guitar music. Sometimes dancers add clicking sounds to the music using hand instruments called castanets.

HIP HOP was created at parties and on the sidewalks of cities. It includes breaking (acrobatic feats), popping (tensing and releasing muscles), and locking (holding positions). Many dancers perform hip hop "freestyle," without a planned choreography, and often have lively competitions with each other.

IRISH STEPDANCE features dancers who hold their upper bodies very still while performing quick steps with their feet, following the lively rhythm of Irish folk music.

JAZZ dance includes torso and hip movements, fancy footwork, large leaps, rapid turns, and energetic movement. This style developed from African dances, tap, and ballet and is often used in musicals.

THE HULA and other Polynesian dances come from the islands of the Pacific Ocean. Dancers wear costumes that include flowers or grass skirts and use hand movements and chants to tell stories and history. The music includes drumming and singing.

TAP involves precise footwork set to the beat of the music. Dancers wear shoes with metal plates on the toes and heels that make tapping noises on wooden floors.

About the Author

Kara Navolio is a freelance writer who tells stories of real-life heroes and interesting people for local newspapers. She loves dancing with her husband or friends, or really any time she hears a good song! Watching other people dance always makes her smile. Kara is the mom of two grown-up kids. She lives in the beautiful San Francisco Bay area, where she works on more books for kids, hikes, paints, and spends time with her family. Visit her online at www.karanavolio.com.

About the Illustrator

Ruth-Mary Smith is an illustrator of children's picture books. Having studied fine arts at TAFE College and participated in watercolor courses over many years, Ruth-Mary enjoys creating images for children to love. Her favorite illustrations can be described as whimsical and sweet. She lives with her three daughters and husband on Sydney's Northern Beaches in Australia. She illustrates from her home studio, working primarily with her favorite medium, watercolors, as well as pastel and pencils. Ruth-Mary greatly enjoyed the opportunity to work on this special project, *Everybody Can Dance!*

CPSIA information can be obtained
at www.ICGtesting.com
Printed in the USA
LVHW011636300523
748407LV00003B/21